# Welcome to Percy's Park!

Percy the park keeper
works hard looking after
the park and his animal
friends who live there.
But Percy still likes to
find time for some fun
and games. And, of
course, in Percy's Park,
there's always time
for a story…

# One Snowy Night

First published in hardback in Great Britain by HarperCollins Publishers Ltd in 1989
First published in paperback by Picture Lions in 1991
New editions published by Collins Picture Books in 2003 and HarperCollins Children's Books in 2011
This edition published in 2019

31 33 35 37 39 40 38 36 34 32

ISBN: 978-0-00-714693-2

Picture Lions and Collins Picture Books are imprints of the Children's Division, part of HarperCollins Publishers Ltd.
HarperCollins Children's Books is a division of HarperCollins Publishers Ltd.

Text and illustrations copyright © Nick Butterworth 1989, 2011, 2019

Visit our website at: www.harpercollins.co.uk

Printed in China

Nick Butterworth

# One Snowy Night

HarperCollins *Children's Books*

It's cold in the park in winter. But Percy the park keeper doesn't mind.

He puts on his warm coat and his big scarf and wears two pairs of woolly socks inside his wellington boots.

Percy likes to be out in the fresh air.

In the middle of the park there is a little hut. This is where Percy lives.

When it gets too cold to be outside, Percy goes into his hut where it's cosy and warm.

T he animals who live in the park all know
Percy's hut. Every day he shares his lunch
with them.

One winter's night it was so cold it began to snow. Great big snowflakes fell past the window of Percy's hut.

"Brr," said Percy. "I think I'll need an extra blanket tonight."

He made himself some hot cocoa and got ready for bed.

Suddenly, Percy heard a tapping sound. There was somebody at the door.

"Now who can that be at this time of night?" thought Percy. He went to the door and looked out.

There on the step was a squirrel. It looked
very cold and miserable.

"I can't get to sleep, Percy," said the squirrel.
"My bed is full of snow."

"Oh dear," said Percy. "Never mind, I've got
plenty of room for two."

The squirrel snuggled down next to Percy
and soon began to feel warm.
Knock! Knock! It was the door again.
"Now who can that be?"
thought Percy.

Standing outside were two shivering rabbits. "It's f-freezing," said one rabbit.

"We're f-frozen," said the other.

"You poor things," said Percy. "Come in and warm up."

The rabbits squeezed into the bed next to Percy and the squirrel. There wasn't much room.

"Could you face the other way?" Percy asked the squirrel. "Your tail is tickling my nose."

Knock! Knock!

"Oh dear," said Percy. "Now there's someone else at the door!"

It was a fox! He looked very cold and hungry. "Can I come in, too?" he asked.

<big>P</big>ercy scratched his head and thought for
a minute.

"Well, if you promise to behave," he said.

"I promise," said the fox, and he squeezed into
bed next to all the other animals.

Bump! Oops! The squirrel fell out.

"Who did that?" asked the squirrel crossly.

Knock, knock, knock!
"Good gracious!" said Percy.
"It's the door again."

This time Percy had quite a surprise.

There on the step were a badger, two ducks,
a hedgehog and a whole family of mice!
They all wanted a bed for the night.

Poor old Percy. And poor old Percy's bed!
The animals pushed and shoved and rolled
around the bed, but there was just not enough
room for them all.

Soon the bed covers ended up in a big, tight ball.

Then, bump! The covers rolled right off the bed and everybody fell on to the floor.

"Oh dear," said Percy. "This won't do at all. My bed is just too small."

Suddenly, one of the mice pricked up his ears.

"What's that noise?" he squeaked.

Everyone listened hard. Now they could all hear it. There was a scratching, scraping sound. It seemed to be coming from underneath them.

"There's something moving under the floor," whispered Percy.

The animals looked frightened and the mice all started to squeak at once.

"Oh dear!"

"What can it be?"

"It might be a monster!"

"With fierce claws!"

"And sharp teeth!"

The noise grew louder and louder. Then, one of the floorboards began to move.

"Look out! It's coming up through the floor!"

Suddenly, there was a loud creak.

"Help!" cried the animals and they all ran to hide.

But Percy wasn't frightened. He started to chuckle. Then he laughed out loud.

A small, dark head was sticking up through the floorboards.

"This isn't a monster," said Percy. "It's a mole!"

"I'm sorry to burst in like this," said the mole. "I knocked on the door but nobody heard me."

Percy helped the mole up through the hole in the floor, sat him on his hot water bottle to get warm and put the floorboard back.

"It's all right everyone," he called. "You can come out now."

But nobody moved. Nobody stirred.
Nobody wanted to come out.

The squirrel was tucked away in the pocket
of Percy's dressing gown.

The hedgehog was in his coat.

The fox…

the rabbits…

the badger…

and the ducks

were all safely hidden away.

The mice had even squeezed themselves into
Percy's slippers!

Everyone had found a cosy bed.

"Well I never!" said Percy.

Percy yawned and snuggled down in his own bed once again.

"That's better. Now I've got plenty of room," he said. "And a little to spare…

…for a mole!"

"I was born in London in 1946 and grew up in a sweet shop in Essex. For several years I worked as a graphic designer, but in 1980 I decided to concentrate on writing and illustrating books for children.

My wife, Annette, and I have a son, Ben, and a daughter, Amanda, and three wonderful grandchildren.

I haven't recently counted how many books there are with my name on the cover but Percy the Park Keeper accounts for a good many of them. I'm reliably informed that they have sold in their millions worldwide. Hooray!

I didn't realise this when I invented Percy, but I can now see that he's very like my mum's dad, my grandpa. Here's a picture of him giving a ride to my mum and my brother, Mike, in his old home-made wheelbarrow!"

Nick Butterworth has presented children's stories on television, worked on a strip for *Sunday Express Magazine* and worked for various major graphic design companies. Among his books published by HarperCollins are *Thud!, QPootle5, Jingle Bells, Albert le Blanc, Tiger* and *The Whisperer,* which won the Nestlé Gold Award. But he is best known for his stories about Percy the Park Keeper, which have sold more than nine million copies worldwide. Percy has also appeared in his own television series.

# Look out for more Percy the Park Keeper stories
## OVER 9 MILLION COPIES SOLD!

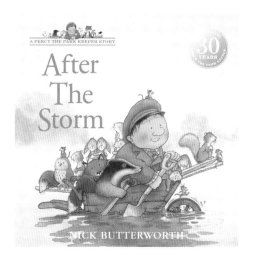

PB: 978-0-00-715515-6

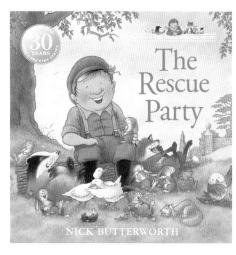

PB: 978-0-00-715516-3

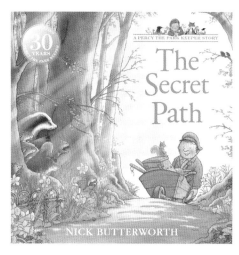

PB: 978-0-00-715518-7

PB: 978-0-00-715517-0

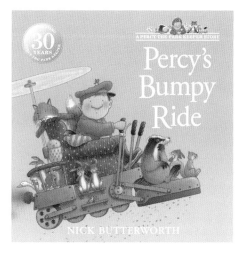

PB: 978-0-00-715514-9

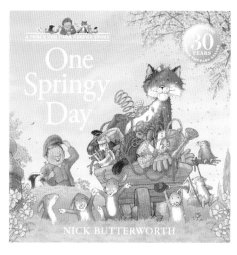

HB: 978-0-00-827986-8

**Percy the Park Keeper stories can be ordered at:**
www.harpercollins.co.uk